GOSCINNY AND UDERZO
PRESENT
AN ASTERIX ADVENTURE

ASTERIX
AND THE
BLACK GOLD

WRITTEN AND ILLUSTRATED BY UDERZO
TRANSLATED BY ANTHEA BELL AND DEREK HOCKRIDGE

HODDER AND STOUGHTON

LONDON   SYDNEY   AUCKLAND   TORONTO

for René

British Library Cataloguing in Publication Data

Goscinny, René
  Asterix and the black gold
  I. Title   II. Uderzo, Albert
  741.5'944   PN6747

English language text copyright © 1982 by
Editions Albert René, Goscinny & Uderzo,
First published in Great Britain 1982 (cased)
Second impression 1982

ISBN 0 340 27476 X

Printed in Belgium for Hodder & Stoughton Children's Books,
a division of Hodder & Stoughton Ltd
Mill Road, Dunton Green, Sevenoaks, Kent TN13 2YJ
by Henri Proost & Cie, Turnhout

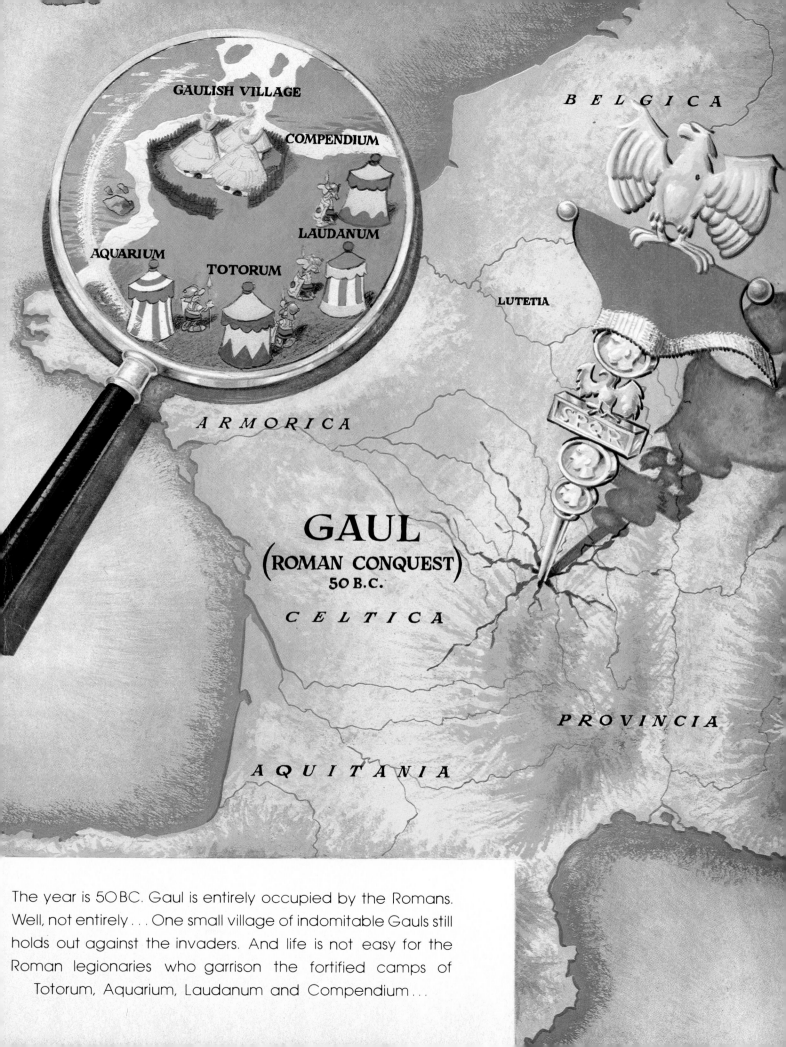

The year is 50 BC. Gaul is entirely occupied by the Romans. Well, not entirely... One small village of indomitable Gauls still holds out against the invaders. And life is not easy for the Roman legionaries who garrison the fortified camps of Totorum, Aquarium, Laudanum and Compendium...

a few of the Gauls

Asterix, the hero of these adventures. A shrewd, cunning little warrior; all perilous missions are immediately entrusted to him. Asterix gets his superhuman strength from the magic potion brewed by the druid Getafix . . .

Obelix, Asterix's inseparable friend. A menhir delivery-man by trade; addicted to wild boar. Obelix is always ready to drop everything and go off on a new adventure with Asterix – so long as there's wild boar to eat, and plenty of fighting. His constant companion is Dogmatix, the only known canine ecologist, who howls with despair when a tree is cut down.

Getafix, the venerable village druid. Gathers mistletoe and brews magic potions. His speciality is the potion which gives the drinker superhuman strength. But Getafix also has other recipes up his sleeve . . .

Cacofonix, the bard. Opinion is divided as to his musical gifts. Cacofonix thinks he's a genius. Everyone else thinks he's unspeakable. But so long as he doesn't speak, let alone sing, everybody likes him . . .

Finally, Vitalstatistix, the chief of the tribe. Majestic, brave and hot-tempered, the old warrior is respected by his men and feared by his enemies. Vitalstatistix himself has only one fear; he is afraid the sky may fall on his head tomorrow. But as he always says, 'Tomorrow never comes.'

IN THE QUIET, PEACEFUL DEPTHS OF THE GAULISH FOREST, EVERYTHING SEEMS TO INDICATE THAT IT IS DINNER TIME...

TAPTAPTAP TAPTAPTAP

SCRUNCH SCRUNCH

...BUT SOME OF THE FOREST DWELLERS HAVE LOST THEIR APPETITES.

OINK! GRUNT! OINK! OINK!

GRUNT! OINK! OINK OINK!

MUNCH! MUNCH!

(AUTHOR'S NOTE: WITH APOLOGIES TO PURISTS, WE PROVIDE A DUBBED VERSION TO FACILITATE YOUR UNDERSTANDING OF THE DIALOGUE.)

ARE YOU QUITE SURE WE AREN'T GOING TO MEET ANY OF THOSE CRAZY GAULS FROM THE VILLAGE?

I TOLD YOU, YOU'RE QUITE SAFE WITH ME. WHY ARE YOU SCARED?

MUNCH! MUNCH!

BECAUSE THEY'VE WOLFED DOWN, SCRUNCHED, CRUNCHED AND GOBBLED UP MY WHOLE HERD, AND I AM THE SOLE SURVIVOR OF A LARGE FAMILY, THAT'S WHY!!!

CALM DOWN! NO NEED TO GO RANTING LIKE A BARNSTORMER*! I ADMIT THEY'RE GOOD AT BRINGING HOME THE BACON...

*HAM ACTOR

...BUT AS WHAT MUST BE CURED CAN'T BE ENDURED, I'VE WORKED OUT AN INFALLIBLE SYSTEM! I'LL BET YOU WE NEVER FEATURE ON THE GAULS' MENU!

AND WHO WINS IF YOU LOSE YOUR BET?

CRAZY GAULS!

DINNER!

IN ROME...

NO, WE MOST CERTAINLY CAN'T HAVE THIS!!!

THAT ARMORICAN VILLAGE IS STILL HOLDING THE MIGHT OF ROME UP TO RIDICULE!

AND I HEAR THAT MY LEGIONS NOW HAVE TO FACE HORDES OF WILD BEASTS!

THE MORALE OF MY TROOPS IS AT ROCK BOTTOM, AND I AM THE LAUGHING STOCK OF MY ENEMIES IN THE SENATE!

AS WE ALL KNOW, WE HAVE FAILED TO CONQUER THOSE INDOMITABLE GAULS BY FORCE, CORRUPTION, OR EVEN KIDNAPPING, AND YET...

3A

M.DEVIUS SURREPTITIUS, YOU'RE CHIEF OF MY SECRET SERVICE, M.I.VI. IF YOU HAVE AN IDEA, BY JUPITER, LET'S HEAR IT!

O CAESAR, THE SECRETS OF THE DRUIDS ARE PASSED ON ONLY FROM DRUID TO DRUID BY WORD OF MOUTH!

WHAT ABOUT IT?

SIMPLE! NO ONE BUT A DRUID WHO IS ALSO SPYING FOR US CAN OBTAIN AND PASS ON THE RECIPE OF THAT MAGIC POTION WHICH MAKES THE GAULS INVINCIBLE!

AND AMONG MY AGENTS I HAVE JUST SUCH A DRUID!

THEN WHAT ARE YOU WAITING FOR? FETCH HIM!

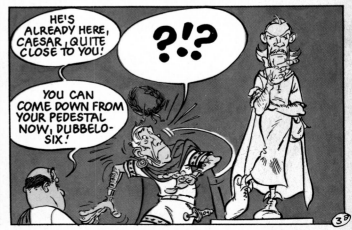

HE'S ALREADY HERE, CAESAR, QUITE CLOSE TO YOU!

?!?

YOU CAN COME DOWN FROM YOUR PEDESTAL NOW, DUBBELO-SIX!

3B

WHAT'S THE IDEA? A SPY, IN MY APARTMENTS?

JUST A LITTLE EXPERIMENT, O CAESAR, TO DEMONSTRATE MY BEST SECRET AGENT'S INVENTIVE GENIUS!

DUBBELOSIX TOOK HIS DRUIDICAL EXAMINATIONS SIX TIMES AND FAILED, HENCE HIS NAME...

AT HIS SEVENTH ATTEMPT THE EXAMINERS, WORN OUT, LET HIM QUALIFY AS A DRUID, AND EVER SINCE, MOTIVATED BY SPITE AND AVARICE, HE HAS BEEN OUR ABLEST DRUIDICAL SPY!

EXCELLENT! BRING ME BACK THE SECRET OF THE MIRACULOUS POTION AND I SHALL FIRE THAT TRYING TRIUMVIRATE, BECOME DICTATOR OF THE WHOLE ROMAN EMPIRE, AND MAKE YOUR FORTUNES!

AVE CAESAR, LUCRATORI TE SALUTANT!*

*HAIL CAESAR, THOSE ABOUT TO GET RICH QUICK SALUTE YOU. 4A

YOU'RE TO SET OFF FOR GAUL AT ONCE. HERE, TAKE THIS...

?

A CARRIER FLY. SHE'S TRAINED TO TAKE MESSAGES, AND IF NEED BE SHE WILL BRING ME INFORMATION BY MICRO-PAPYRUS IN RECORD TIME!*

* THE EARLIEST KNOWN USE OF A BUG IN ESPIONAGE.

AND HERE'S A SCROLL OF SECRET INSTRUCTIONS, TO BE READ WHEN YOU HAVE LEFT THE CITY OF ROME!

BZZZ!

HOW ARE YOU PLANNING TO TRAVEL?

THAT'S TAKEN CARE OF. WATCH THIS!

CLICK!

CLINK! CLONK! CLICK! CLACK!

CLANG!

I HAVEN'T MANAGED TO FOLD UP THE HORSES UP IN IT YET, THOUGH!

4B

LATER... WHOA! TIME TO READ SURREPTITIUS'S SECRET INSTRUCTIONS!

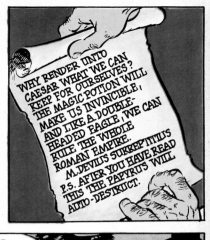

WHY RENDER UNTO CAESAR WHAT WE CAN KEEP FOR OURSELVES? THE MAGIC POTION WILL MAKE US INVINCIBLE, AND LIKE A DOUBLE-HEADED EAGLE, WE CAN RULE THE WHOLE ROMAN EMPIRE. M.DEVIUS SURREPTITIUS P.S. AFTER YOU HAVE READ THIS THE PAPYRUS WILL AUTO-DESTRUCT.

?!

PSSCHCHCH...

HO, HO! CAESAR AND SURREPTITIUS ARE A COUPLE OF FOOLS! I PLAN TO BE A VULTURE RULING THE GALLO-ROMAN EMPIRE ALONE!

BZZZZ
KISS!

OH LEAVE ME ALONE, YOU WRETCHED CREATURE!

BZ ZZZ ZZ Z

5A

MEANWHILE, ON THE ARMORICAN COAST, ALL IS PEACEFUL IN THE LITTLE GAULISH VILLAGE WHERE ASTERIX AND HIS FRIENDS LIVE.

IT'S A FUNNY THING, BUT WHEN WE GO WILD BOAR-HUNTING THESE DAYS WE KEEP FINDING ROMAN PATROLS!

YES, YOU'D THINK THEY'D KNOW BY NOW BOAR IS ONE OF OUR SACRED COWS! SCRUNCH!

AND YOU CERTAINLY GO THE WHOLE HOG EATING IT!

SCRUNCH! MUNCH! SCRUNCH!

5B

IT WILL BE TERRIBLE IF HE DOESN'T COME, TERRIBLE!

APPALLING!

GHASTLY!

CATASTROPHIC!

SLAM!

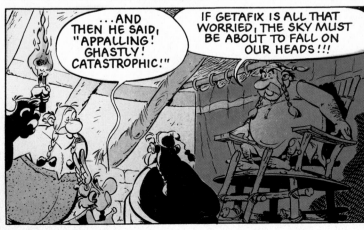

...AND THEN HE SAID, "APPALLING! GHASTLY! CATASTROPHIC!"

IF GETAFIX IS ALL THAT WORRIED, THE SKY MUST BE ABOUT TO FALL ON OUR HEADS!!!

SO FAR, HOWEVER, NOTHING BUT NIGHT HAS FALLEN ON THE VILLAGE AND ITS PEOPLE, SOME OF WHOM ARE IN FOR TROUBLED DREAMS.

BUT NEXT MORNING...

COME QUICKLY! EKONOMIKRISIS THE PHOENICIAN MERCHANT HAS LANDED ON THE BEACH!!!

HE'S HERE! AT LAST!!

HULLO, ASTERIX! NICE DAY, ISN'T IT?

?!

I WOULDN'T MIND TASTING YOUR NEW BARREL OF BEER, VITALSTATISTIX! DON'T FORGET!

?!

8A

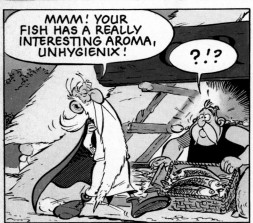

MMM! YOUR FISH HAS A REALLY INTERESTING AROMA, UNHYGIENIX!

?!?

SO GETAFIX WAS WAITING FOR EKONOMIKRISIS AND HIS CARGO!

AND HE APPRECIATED MY FISH, SO THERE!

THAT'S WHAT WORRIES ME. ANYONE IN THAT STATE MUST BE ON THE BRINK OF SUICIDE!

HERE YOU ARE AT LAST, EKONOMIKRISIS, OLD CHAP!

HULLO THERE, GETAFIX! I'VE BEEN LOOKING FORWARD TO SEEING YOU ALL AGAIN EVER SINCE MY LAST VOYAGE! LOOK WHAT I'VE BROUGHT FROM TYRE, SPECIALLY FOR YOU!

8B

AND OF COURSE YOU'VE BROUGHT WHAT I ORDERED WHEN YOU LAST PUT IN HERE?

REMIND ME WHAT IT WAS, WILL YOU?

ROCK OIL, OF COURSE!

BY THE GREAT GOD BAAL! I KNEW I'D FORGOTTEN SOMETHING!!!

SLAP!

WHAAAT?

NOW DON'T GET WORKED UP! I CAN LET YOU HAVE PURPLE, INCENSE, SPICES, PRECIOUS STONES...

NOOO! I WANT ROCK OIL! I ABSOLUTELY MUST HAVE...

THUMP! THUMP! THUMP! THUMP!

AAARRGH!

BOING!

IT'S A STROKE. I'VE SEEN THIS BEFORE. MY BROTHER-IN-LAW HAD ONE WHEN THE ROMAN QUAESTOR SENT HIM HIS TAX DEMAND!

QUICK, OBELIX, LET'S CARRY HIM TO HIS HUT!

I'M SO SORRY! BUT WHY WOULD ANY-ONE GET INTO SUCH A STATE OVER COMMON ROCK OIL?

WHAT'S ROCK OIL?

OIL WHICH GUSHES OUT OF ROCKY GROUND, HENCE ITS NAME. IT'S FOUND MAINLY IN MESOPOTAMIA, AND IS ALSO CALLED NAPHTHA.

AND WHAT'S SO SPECIAL ABOUT THIS OIL?

NOTHING! YOU CAN BURN IT IN AN OIL LAMP, BUT IT SMELLS SO BAD NO ONE USES IT MUCH.

I'M WORRIED! HE DOESN'T SEEM TO BE IMPROVING, AND WE CAN'T DOSE HIM WITH MAGIC POTION BECAUSE WE'VE RUN OUT. GO AND LOOK FOR ANOTHER DRUID TO TREAT HIM, ASTERIX!

BUT WHAT'S THIS OIL GOT TO DO WITH OUR POTION?

IT IS ONE OF THE POTION'S MANY INGREDIENTS, AND I'M SORRY TO SAY I HAVEN'T GOT A SINGLE DROP LEFT!

BZZZ!

CLAP!

HELP! MY FLY!

NOW, ALTHOUGH I NEED ONLY ONE DROP OF ROCK OIL FOR THE POTION, THAT ONE DROP IS ABSOLUTELY ESSENTIAL!

MISSED!

BZZZZZ!

PHEW!

BUT THIS IS TERRIBLE! WHAT'S TO BECOME OF US? THERE'LL BE NO ONE BUT OBELIX LEFT TO DEFEND THE VILLAGE!

BECAUSE AS EVERYONE KNOWS, I FELL INTO THE CAULDRON OF MAGIC POTION WHEN I WAS A BABY AND IT HAD A PERMANENT EFFECT ON ME AND BLAH BLAH BLAH...

?!

BZZ

?!

?!

?!

14A

HUH! WE'VE BEEN IN WORSE TROUBLE BEFORE! WITH OUR CHIEF'S PERMISSION, I'LL GO TO MESOPOTAMIA AND BRING SOME ROCK OIL BACK!

WHAT ABOUT ME?

YOU'RE STAYING HERE TO DEFEND THE VILLAGE IN CASE THE ROMANS ATTACK!

OH NO, I'M NOT! I WANT TO GO TO METOPO... MESOTO... WELL, THE PLACE WHERE ROCKS GUSH OUT OF THE OIL TOO!

OBELIX IS RIGHT! SUCH A LONG AND DANGEROUS JOURNEY MAY PRESENT PROBLEMS. TWO MEN SHOULD GO!

MEANWHILE, LET'S HOPE CAESAR'S SPIES DON'T FIND OUT HOW WEAK WE ARE!

CAESAR WOULD PAY HANDSOMELY FOR THIS INFORMATION, BUT I THINK I CAN DO BETTER!

BZZZZ

14B

EKOMOMIKRISIS, CAN YOU TAKE US TO FIND ROCK OIL?

NOT UNTIL I'VE SOLD OFF MY STOCK, ASTERIX.

OBELIX AND I WILL SELL YOUR STOCK ON THE WAY!

ALL RIGHT, THEN!

GETAFIX, I AM A DRUID TOO! WOULD YOU GIVE ME THE RECIPE FOR THE MAGIC POTION?

HMM... WHAT WOULD YOU DO WITH IT?

OH, JUST HELP THE WEAK AND THE OPPRESSED A BIT!

MAYBE... IF I CAN'T GET HOLD OF ALL THE INGREDIENTS FOR THE RECIPE...

...BUT I'M SURE ASTERIX WILL BRING ME BACK SOME ROCK OIL!

SO I MUST MAKE SURE ASTERIX'S MISSION FAILS!!!

BZZZ!

YOU'RE QUITE RIGHT, GETAFIX! I SHOULD LIKE TO CONTRIBUTE TO THE SUCCESS OF THIS VENTURE MYSELF! IF NO ONE MINDS, I'LL GO TO MESOPOTAMIA WITH ASTERIX AND OBELIX!

BZZZ!

15A

THE DAY OF DEPARTURE COMES.

AND REMEMBER THE FATE OF THE VILLAGE IS IN YOUR HANDS! WITHOUT POTION, WE HAVEN'T GOT A LEG TO STAND ON!

OR A SHIELD, FATTY!

HERE, ASTERIX! LUCKILY I KEPT THIS GOURD OF MAGIC POTION IN RESERVE!

AND KEEP AN EYE ON DUBBELOSIX! SOMETHING TELLS ME NOT TO TRUST HIM!

DON'T WORRY, I'LL WATCH HIM!

I WILL NOW GIVE YOU...

YOU JUST TRY IT!

BUT WHERE'S DUBBELOSIX?

15B

20

AND JUST THEN...

SAIL AHOY, MR OPERATOR!

...A ROMAN GALLEY SAILS INTO THEIR KEN.

PHOENICIAN SHIP AHEAD!

IT MUST BE THE ONE CARRYING THOSE INDOMITABLE GAULS WE HEARD ABOUT!

NOW FOR A GREAT DISPLAY OF NAVAL OPERATIONS, ROMAN FASHION! MY *MAGNUM OPUS!* *

REMEMBER CAESAR WANTS THIS OP TO SUCCEED, CAPTAIN!

*IN FACT, THE CAPTAIN'S OP. No.1

GOODY! ROMANS! NOW FOR SOME FUN AT LAST!

SOMETHING TELLS ME THEY'RE NOT HERE FOR FUN!

THE FLY HAS DELIVERED MY MESSAGE ALL RIGHT! WELL DONE THE SECRET SERVICE!

CLAP! CLAP! CLAP!

WE NOW HAVE A CHANCE TO OBSERVE THE SUPERBLY EFFICIENT BOARDING TACTICS PRACTISED BY THE ROMAN NAVY. FIRST, BALLISTAE THROW OUT GRAPPLING HOOKS...

WHOOSH!

WHOOSH!

THEN THE ROMANS SIMPLY PULL, AND THE ENEMY'S FAT IS IN THE FIRE!

WHAT DO YOU MEAN, THE ENEMY'S FAT?

WHÓOOSH!

BOING!

SHALL WE GET THEM, OBELIX?

LET'S GET THEM, ASTERIX!

BOARD 'EM!

YOU CAN'T DO THAT! THAT'S A FOUL!

WE ARE BOARDING YOU, SEE?

PIF PAF!

ALWAYS THE SAME OLD STORY: AS SOON AS THEY FEEL THEY'RE OUTNUMBERED THE ROMANS WON'T PLAY!

♪ FAREWELL AND ADIEU TO YOU BOLD ROMAN SOLDIERS, FAREWELL AND ADIEU TO YOU SOLDIERS OF ROME... ♪

BONG!

FLAP!

GRRR.!

BAM!

WHAT A SHAME I'VE NOTHING LEFT TO SELL!

THESE WATER SPORTS REALLY PEP THINGS UP!

IT'S NOT TRUE! IT JUST ISN'T TRUE!!!

BUT IT IS! AND SOON AFTERWARDS...

SAID IT WAS HIS MAGNUM OPUS, THE FOOL!

GLUG! GLUG! GLUG! GLUG!

I FEAR THAT WAS MY NAVAL OP. No. 1st AND LAST!

AND ONCE AGAIN...

ROMAN GALLEY AHOY, MR OPERATOR.

...THE NOW CLASSIC BOARDING TACTICS...

BONG!

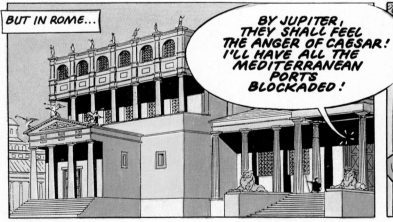

...ARE FOLLOWED BY AN EQUALLY TRADITIONAL FIGHT AND ITS AFTERMATH.

WE'RE HAVING FUN, AREN'T WE, ASTERIX?

YES, BUT IT SEEMS ODD FOR THE ROMANS TO BE SO KEEN ON FIGHTING US, OBELIX!

BANG!

BIFF!

BING!

PAF!

EVERY TIME I SEE IT AGAIN I FIND SOMETHING ELSE TO APPRECIATE!

BUT IN ROME...

BY JUPITER, THEY SHALL FEEL THE ANGER OF CAESAR! I'LL HAVE ALL THE MEDITERRANEAN PORTS BLOCKADED!

AND LOOK SHARP! I DON'T EXPECT MY NAVAL COMMANDERS TO STOP AND CONTEMPLATE ANY NAVELS!*

*POPULAR MEDITERRANEAN FRUIT

I WANT TO MAKE SURE NOT EVEN A FLY COULD GET THROUGH THE NET!

HM...AND THINKING OF FLIES...

SURREPTITIUS!

ANY NEWS OF YOUR AGENT DUBBEL... DUBBEL SOMETHING?

I'M AFRAID WE HAVE A COMMUNICATIONS PROBLEM, O CAESAR!

PROBLEM? WHAT SORT OF PROBLEM?

OUR CARRIER FLY IS GOING SLOW, AND IF SHE ACTUALLY GOES ON STRIKE...

WELL, IF IT'S WILDLIFE WE'RE DISCUSSING, HOW WOULD YOU LIKE TO FIND OUT IF THE LIONS IN THE CIRCUS ARE ON HUNGER STRIKE?!!!

BONK!

I MUST TRY TO ENTICE HER BACK...

WHERE'S A PRETTY FLY, THEN..?

HONEY

BZZZ ZZZZZZ

BZZZZZZZZZZ

BZZZZ ZZZZZ

I MIGHT HAVE KNOWN IT!

HONEY

EMERGING FROM ITS NAVAL CAMPAIGN, THE PHOENICIAN SHIP SAILS PEACEFULLY ON ITS WAY.

GAUL

ITALY

GREECE

MESOPOTAMIA

HISPANIA

TYRE

EGYPT

ASTERIX, I'M TIRED OF THIS VOYAGE, AND I GET HUNGRY WHEN I'M TIRED!

WAIT A BIT LONGER, OBELIX. WE SHOULD SOON BE LANDING AT TYRE!

DON'T TIRE NOW, HERE COMES TYRE!

BUT ONE OF THE FINEST OF PHOENICIAN TRADING PORTS HAS BECOME INACCESSIBLE. THE HARBOUR MOUTH IS BLOCKED BY BIREMES, TRIREMES, QUADRIREMES AND QUINQUIREMES.

26

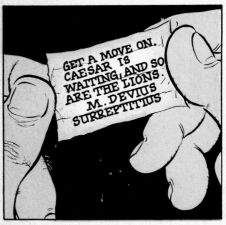

28

NEXT MORNING...

THERE'S THE PROMISED LAND, ASTERIX!

GO TO JERUSALEM AND TELL SAMSON ALIUS I SENT YOU. HE'S MY SUPPLIER: YOU'LL BE ABLE TO GET ROCK OIL FROM HIM.

THANKS, EKONOMI-KRISIS! SEE YOU SOON, MAYBE!

I HOPE SO! TRAVELLING WITH YOU IS AN ENRICHING EXPERIENCE!

AND I'M STILL HUNGRY! DO YOU THINK THERE ARE ANY WILD BOARS HERE?

NEVER MIND THAT. WE'VE GOT TO FIND OUR WAY!

THERE'S SOMEONE WHO MIGHT BE ABLE TO HELP US!

HULLO, FRIEND! CAN YOU TELL US THE WAY TO JERUSALEM?

MY DONKEY AND I ARE GOING THERE OUR-SELVES! LET'S JOIN FORCES!

MY NAME'S JOSHUA BEN ZEDRIN.

I'M ASTERIX. MEET OBELIX, DOGMATIX, AND DUBBELOSIX THE DRUID!

WE'VE COME FROM GAUL TO BUY ROCK OIL FROM THE MERCHANT SAMSON ALIUS.

I WOULDN'T HAVE THOUGHT ANYONE WOULD COME SO FAR FOR THAT!

ARE THERE MANY ROMANS HERE?

NOT AS MANY AS IN PHOENICIA. THAT'S A ROMAN PROVINCE. WE'RE ONLY A PROTECTORATE, AND THE ROMANS DON'T HAVE A STRONG GARRISON IN JERUSALEM!

A LITTLE LATER...

LET'S STOP AND CAMP HERE!

DO YOU THINK THAT MEANS IT'S DINNER TIME, ASTERIX?

YOU CAN SHARE MY MEAL, THOUGH I HAVE NOTHING BUT DRIED FRUIT TO OFFER!

WE WOULDN'T LIKE TO DEPRIVE YOU!

NO WILD BOAR? EVEN DRIED WOULD DO.

WHAT'S WILD BOAR?

SINGULARIS PORCUS, GENUS OF PACHYDERMOUS UNGULATE MAMMALS OF WHICH THIS SPECIES INHABITS GAUL AND IS SIMPLY DELICIOUS!

?!

PORK?!! WE ARE FORBIDDEN TO EAT PORK BY THE LAW AND THE PROPHETS!*

*LEVITICUS 11, vii

PROFITS? YOU MEAN PORK BUTCHERS CAN'T MAKE A PROFIT HERE?

26A

AT LAST, AFTER SEVERAL DAYS ON THE ROAD, OUR FRIENDS ARRIVE IN JERUSALEM, THE GREAT ROYAL CITY BEHIND ITS HIGH WALLS, LATER TO OPEN ITS GATES TO ALL THE FAITHS OF THE WORLD.

26B

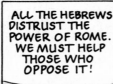

BUT WE MUST TAKE SOME ROCK OIL BACK TO GAUL! IT'S VITAL!

THEN YOU'LL HAVE TO LOOK WHERE THEY FIND IT: NEAR BABYLON IN MESOPOTAMIA!

HOW MANY MILES TO BABYLON?

WELL, IT'S THIRTY DAYS' JOURNEY, AND YOU'LL HAVE TO CROSS THE DESERT!

I'VE NEVER TRIED A DESERT CROSSING BEFORE, BUT BY TOUTATIS, I'M READY TO TACKLE IT!

HERE'S MY ASSISTANT, SAUL BEN EPHISHUL. AT SUNRISE HE WILL GUIDE YOU TO THE EDGE OF THE DESERT.

WEAR THESE AND YOU'LL PASS UNNOTICED.

HOW CAN WE THANK YOU?

OH, IF YOU'RE AIMING TO GIVE THE ROMANS TROUBLE, WE'RE QUITS!

BUT YOUR OWN NAME SOUNDS RATHER ROMAN, SAMSON ALIUS?

I TOOK THIS ALIAS FOR BUSINESS REASONS. MY REAL NAME IS ROSEN-BLUMENTHALOVITCH!

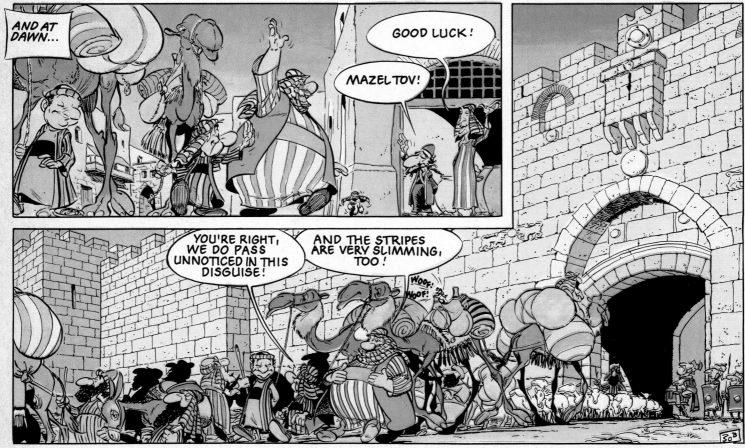

AND AT DAWN...

GOOD LUCK!

MAZEL TOV!

YOU'RE RIGHT, WE DO PASS UNNOTICED IN THIS DISGUISE!

AND THE STRIPES ARE VERY SLIMMING, TOO!

WOOF! WOOF!

AT THE ROMAN PROCURATOR'S PALACE...

AVE, O PONTIUS PIRATE! THE GAULS GOT AWAY, AND WE FEAR THEY'VE MADE GOOD THEIR ESCAPE NOW!

ONCE THEY'RE OUTSIDE MY TERRITORY, MY DEAR DUBBEL-OSIX, I COULDN'T CARE LESS WHAT THEY DO!

I WISH HE'D STOP WASHING HIS HANDS THE WHOLE TIME!

WELL, NEVER MIND! ASTERIX AND OBELIX ARE BOUND TO GO BACK ON BOARD SHIP, AND WHEN THEY DO WE'LL BE WAITING, WITH QUITE A RECEPTION COMMITTEE!

MEANWHILE...

WE'RE COMING TO THE DEAD SEA!

IT MAKES ME SICK, ASTERIX!

I HAVE TO ADMIT THESE MOUNTS ARE RATHER BUMPY!

I DIDN'T MEAN THAT! IT MAKES ME SICK TO THINK OF THE RACIAL DISCRIMI— NATION PRACTISED AGAINST BOARS IN THIS COUNTRY!

?!?

THE SEA! YIPPEE!!!

IT'S SO HOT, I COULD DO WITH A NICE DIP!

HEY, WAIT!

HERE GOES!

?

FLOP! FLOP! FLOP! FLOP!

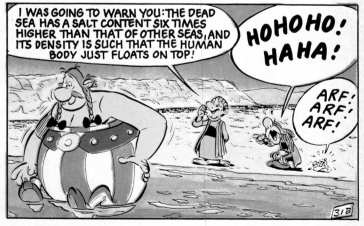

I WAS GOING TO WARN YOU: THE DEAD SEA HAS A SALT CONTENT SIX TIMES HIGHER THAN THAT OF OTHER SEAS, AND ITS DENSITY IS SUCH THAT THE HUMAN BODY JUST FLOATS ON TOP!

HO HO HO! HA HA!

ARF! ARF! ARF!

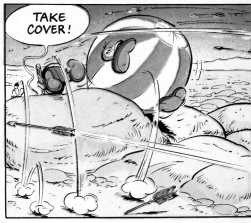

39

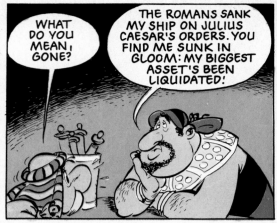

44

BUT... BUT THEY'RE FIGHTING! *WITHOUT POTION!!*

WITHOUT US EITHER. IT'S NOT FAIR!

GETAFIX, WHAT IS THIS MIRACLE? WHAT'S GOING ON?

HULLO, ASTERIX, HAD A NICE TRIP?

I'M AFRAID I HAVEN'T BROUGHT ANY ROCK OIL BACK, GETAFIX!

ANY WHAT OIL?

ROCK OIL, OF COURSE! BLACK GOLD! THE VITAL INGREDIENT OF THE MAGIC POTION!

OH, YES, PETRA OLEUM!

DON'T WORRY! FORTUNATELY, AFTER CONDUCTING A FEW EXPERIMENTS, I MANAGED TO SUBSTITUTE BEETROOT JUICE INSTEAD. WE RUN JUST AS WELL ON BEETROOT JUICE, AND IT TASTES NICER!

BONK!

?.

43A

IT'S A STROKE! I'VE SEEN THIS BEFORE. MY BROTHER-IN-LAW HAD ONE WHEN...

WANT ME TO THUMP YOU?

GO AWAY! I'LL TREAT HIM FOR SHOCK.

YOU'RE RIGHT. THE NEW MAGIC POTION DOES TASTE NICER, BUT ANOTHER TIME I WISH YOU'D CONDUCT YOUR EXPERIMENTS BEFORE SENDING US TO THE ENDS OF THE EARTH, GETAFIX!

I WILL, ASTERIX!

HEY, ASTERIX, WHAT SHALL WE DO WITH THESE TWO?

WHAT WITH ALL THE EXCITEMENT I'D ALMOST FORGOTTEN THEM!

IS DUBBELOSIX'S CHARIOT STILL AROUND?

DON'T MENTION THAT CHARIOT TO ME! I TRIED USING IT, AND IT TURNED INTO A TRUNK! I WAS SHUT INSIDE IT FOR THREE DAYS BEFORE ANYONE COULD GET ME OUT!

EXACTLY WHAT I NEED!

43B

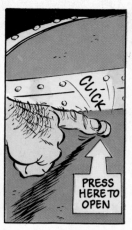

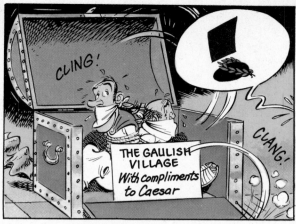

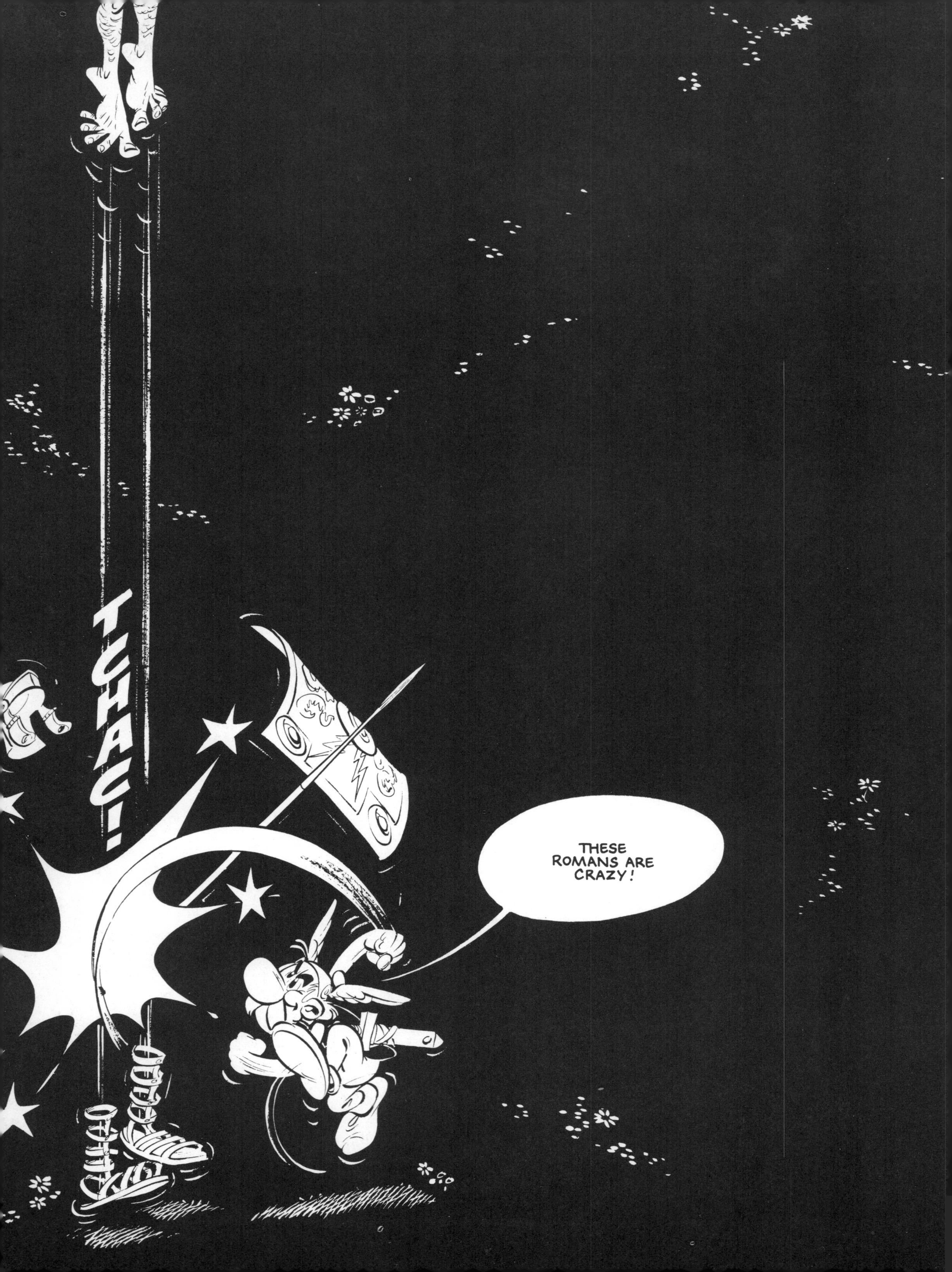
TCHAC!
THESE ROMANS ARE CRAZY!